Dear PILLOW

written by
Susan Saunders Lehrer

To Alex and Molly, my two wonderful daughters who
always go to bed on time, and to my dear husband, Scott,
who definitely does not snore.

S.S.L.

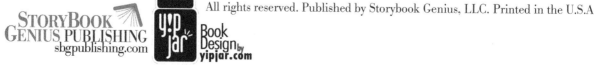

One night, like many nights before,
Charlie lay awake in his bed.

Tossing.
Turning.
Blankets on.
Blankets off.

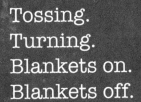

Charlie could not
get to sleep, again.
But on this night,
Charlie had an idea.

Hello Charlie,

Sorry it's hard for you to fall asleep, but how can you be bored? There is much to do around here! For starters, I need help with Bear. He does not stop talking. While you are at school, all I hear about is the time somebody ate Bear's porridge. And the day Bear went over the mountain. His stories go on. And on. It's unbearable. I work nights, so it's important that I get my daytime rest. Please find Bear another friend who can listen to his stories.

Pillow

P.S. Of course I can read! I read over, under and around your shoulders every night.

blah blah blah

So Charlie searched and searched
until he found a perfect
new friend for Bear.

Dear Charlie,

Thanks for taking care of Bear,
but something else has come up.
And down.
And up.

Basketball bounces ALL DAY LONG—scoring Pillow a giant headache. Please find Basketball another place to get his "bouncies" out.

Pillow

So Charlie chased
Basketball out of his room.
Down the stairs.
Through the living room.
And all around the kitchen.

Charlie finally **caught**
Basketball, brought him
to the basement and put
him on the highest shelf his
arms could reach.

Psst...Pillow,

Are you up? I fell asleep, but a scary dream woke me up. Lucky for me, you were in my dream, too. Together we fought off a flock of flying cheeseburgers!

Charlie

P.S. Do pillows have scary dreams?

Dear Charlie,

Yikes, that does sound scary. Good thing cheeseburger dreams are pretty rare. Happy to help. Rest assured, my job is to support you every way I can!

Pillow

P.S. Everyone has a scary dream once in a while. Even pillows! Just the other day I dreamed that you left me at Grandma's house.

Dear Charlie,

Although Monkey and I make a great pair, he does not have the best, uh... what I am trying to say is that Monkey STINKS! It's hard to relax when I have to hold my nose all day. Please give Monkey a much-needed bath.

Pillow

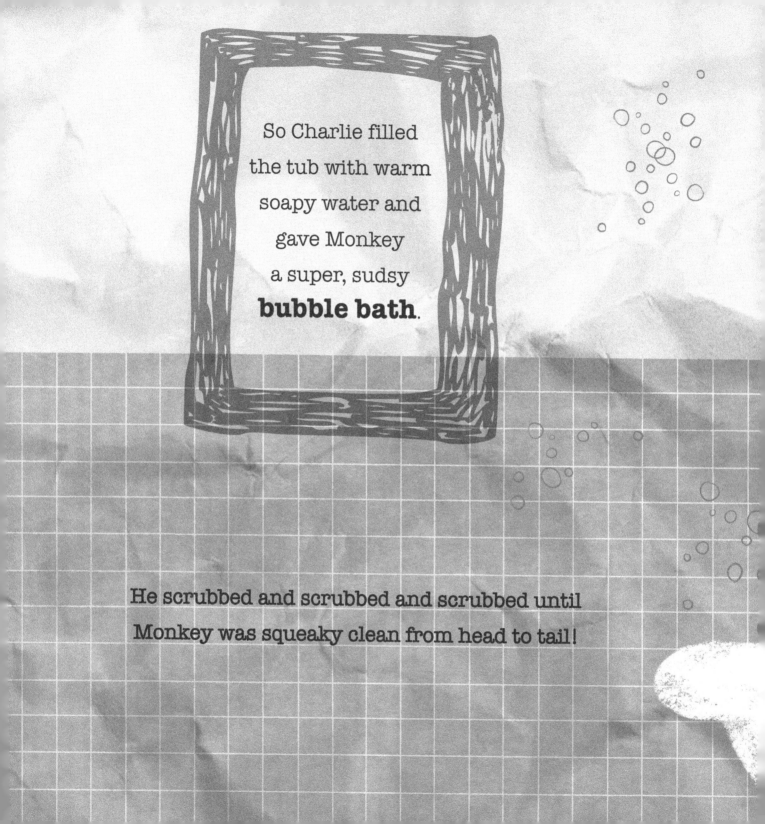

So Charlie filled
the tub with warm
soapy water and
gave Monkey
a super, sudsy
bubble bath.

He scrubbed and scrubbed and scrubbed until
Monkey was squeaky clean from head to tail!

Dear Charlie,

I don't want to be a snitch, but your little sister comes into your room when you are not home. She plays with all of your toys and makes a ton of noise. I think we both agree this needs to stop.

Pillow

Not happy with this news, Charlie built a special trap that would keep his little sister **out** of his room. For good!

blah blah blah blah blah blah blah blah blah blah

DEAR PILLOW:

Bear has a new friend.

Basketball is tucked far away in the basement.

score!

Dear Charlie,

At first I thought a big storm was rolling in, but no, it was your snoring! Can you keep it down? I'm trying to do my job in peace. Thank you for all of your help. Now we can both get the rest we need! Goodnight, Charlie.

Pillow

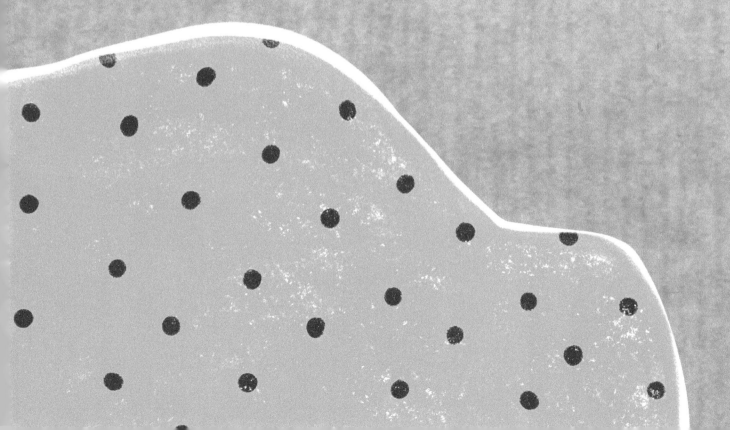

One night, like many nights before,
Charlie sat at the dinner table
staring at his plate.

Push peas to the right.
Slide yucky chicken to the left.
Charlie did not like his dinner.

But on this night, Charlie had an idea.

Dear Plate...